NELLIE BELLE

written by
Mem Fox

illustrated by
Mike Austin

BEACH LANE BOOKS • New York London Toronto Sydney New Delhi

Is it fun in the yard,
Nellie Belle, Nellie Belle?

Is it fun in the yard,
Nellie Belle?

Digging earth
that's very hard,

in the yard,

in the yard—

is it fun in the yard, Nellie Belle?

Is it fun in the street,
Nellie Belle, Nellie Belle?
Is it fun in the street,
Nellie Belle?

Greeting everyone
you meet,

in the street,

in the street—

is it fun in the street, Nellie Belle?

Is it fun on the beach, Nellie Belle, Nellie Belle?
Is it fun on the beach, Nellie Belle?

With the seagulls
out of reach,

on the beach,

on the beach—

is it fun on the beach, Nellie Belle?

Is it fun in the sea, Nellie Belle, Nellie Belle?
Is it fun in the sea, Nellie Belle?

Swimming fast
and swimming free,

in the sea,

in the sea—

is it fun in the sea, Nellie Belle?

Is it fun in the park, Nellie Belle, Nellie Belle?

Is it fun in the park, Nellie Belle?

Seeing possums in the dark,
in the park, in the park—
is it fun in the park, Nellie Belle?

It's best on the *bed*,
Nellie Belle, Nellie Belle!

It's best on the *bed*, Nellie Belle.

Snuggled up
to dear old Ted,

on the bed,

on the bed—

snuggled up to dear old Ted . . .

Nellie Belle!

For Pam Witton, dog lover—M. F.

For Tien and Reid—M. A.

 BEACH LANE BOOKS

An imprint of Simon & Schuster Children's Publishing Division • 1230 Avenue of the Americas, New York, New York 10020 • Text copyright © 2015 by Mem Fox • Illustrations copyright © 2015 by Michael Austin • All rights reserved, including the right of reproduction in whole or in part in any form. • BEACH LANE BOOKS is a trademark of Simon & Schuster, Inc. • For information about special discounts for bulk purchases, please contact Simon & Schuster Special Sales at 1-866-506-1949 or business@simonandschuster.com. • The Simon & Schuster Speakers Bureau can bring authors to your live event. For more information or to book an event, contact the Simon & Schuster Speakers Bureau at 1-866-248-3049 or visit our website at www.simonspeakers.com.
Book design by Lauren Rille
The text for this book is set in Archer.
The illustrations for this book are rendered digitally.
Manufactured in China
0915 SCP
First Edition
10 9 8 7 6 5 4 3 2 1
Library of Congress Cataloging-in-Publication Data
Fox, Mem, 1946– author.
Nellie Belle / Mem Fox ; illustrated by Mike Austin.—First edition.
p. cm.
Nellie Belle, a puppy, has fun from morning to night.
ISBN 978-1-4169-9005-5 (hardcover : alk. paper)
ISBN 978-1-4391-5724-4 (eBook)
[1. Stories in rhyme. 2. Dogs—Fiction. 3. Animals—Infancy—Fiction.]
I. Austin, Mike, 1963– illustrator. II. Title.
PZ8.3.F8245Nel 2015
[E]—dc23
2014042902